Stories to Share

Stories to Share

tiger tales

Contents

Follow That Bear
If You DARE!

by Claire Freedman

Illustrated by
Alison Edgson

Hare loved bears.

He liked big bears, little bears, hairy bears, and scary bears.

"If only I could find a bear," said Hare. "If only I could catch one! The hairier and scarier, the better!"

So Hare bought a book:
The Best Book of Bear Hunting.
He opened his book
and took a look.

STEP 1

BEAR HUNTING

A WARNING
(please read carefully)

WHEN going on a hunt, to find a bear, you need to take the utmost care.

It's best to take a friend along, too — choose one who's as excited as you!

"Rabbit!" called Hare. "I need you
for a Very Important Bear Hunt!"

"A Bear Hunt?" said Rabbit. "How
do you hunt for bears?"

"It's all in my book," explained Hare. So he
turned the page, and they took a look.

STEP 2

THINGS YOU WILL NEED

TO catch your bear, take a fishing net, some string — as long as you can get —

	L	S	D
~~	20	0	0
~~	10	5	2
~~	0	2	4
~~	30	7	6

A FLASHLIGHT to shine inside his lair, and watchful eyes for

BEARS LURK EVERYWHERE!

"Are you sure you want to find a bear, Hare?" said Rabbit.

"Of course!" Hare said. "The hairier and scarier, the better! Look, I've found a fishing net, a flashlight, and a piece of string. What's next?"

They turned another page in Hare's book and took a look.

STEP 3

TRAILING YOUR BEAR

Now bears are not always easily found, so look for pawprints on the ground.

Crouch down low but please beware –

THE BIGGER THE PAWPRINT, THE BIGGER THE BEAR!

"I don't think I like the sound of Bear Hunting," said Rabbit anxiously. "I hope we don't find any bear prints!"

"Over here!" called Hare excitedly. "I've found some!"

"Oh, dear!" said Rabbit. "They must belong to a VERY hairy, scary bear. Now what?"

They turned another page
of Hare's book and took a look.

STEP 4

WHAT TO LOOK FOR

BEARS like to scratch on a favorite tree, it sharpens their claws as sharp as can be!

THEIR nails stay as sharp as the teeth in their jaws.

The deeper the scratch marks, the sharper the claws!

"I really don't like the idea of Bear Hunting!" cried Rabbit. "Let's go back!"

"Not now!" cried Hare excitedly. "We're on the trail! And look what I've found!"

Rabbit looked. "Oh, no!" he cried. "Now what do we do?"

"I'll tell you," said Hare. "It's all in my book."

So they turned another
page and took a look.

GETTING CLOSER AND CLOSER

WHEN a bear is close,
you may hear grumbling;
that is the sound
of his tummy rumbling.

HIDE yourself quickly and take great care—

the louder the rumble,
the hungrier the bear!

Rumble
Grumble!

"Shh! Did you hear that?" whispered
Hare excitedly. "That sounds like a
very hungry bear to me!"
"*Hear* it?" trembled Rabbit.
"I was almost deafened by it! Quick,
Hare, let's take another look in
your book!"

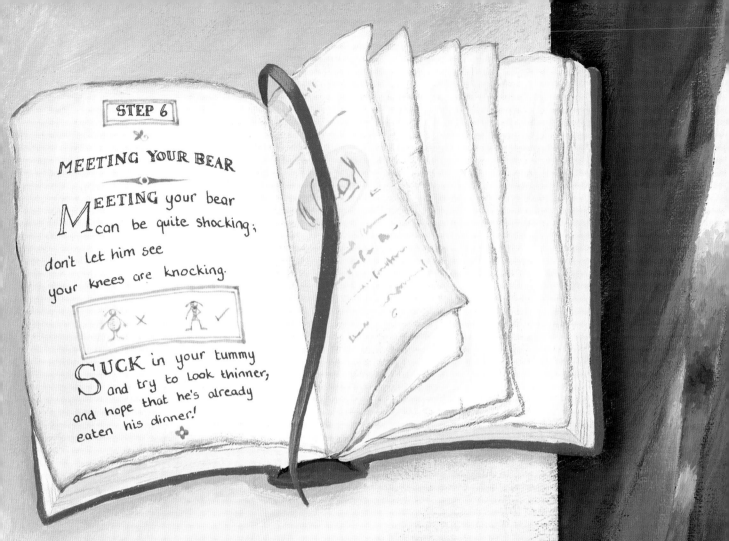

STEP 6

MEETING YOUR BEAR

MEETING your bear
can be quite shocking;
don't let him see
your knees are knocking.

SUCK in your tummy
and try to look thinner,
and hope that he's already
eaten his dinner!

"Yikes!" gulped Rabbit. "Look over there, Hare!"

"Where?"

"It's a BEAR!"

"HELP! We'll never catch HIM with a fishing net and a piece of string!" trembled Rabbit.

"Just watch me try!" cried Hare.

"I'm HUNGRY!" growled the bear.

Then, suddenly . . .

"Dinner's ready," called Mommy Bear.
"It's bear-sized beans on bear-sized toast."
"Yummy!" said Little Bear. "Must go!"

"Come back!" called Hare.
Poor Rabbit was too weak to speak!
"Oh, no," cried Hare. "I can't lose
my bear—that's not fair!"

Quickly he took another look in his book.

STEP 7

WHAT BEARS LIKE TO EAT

A HUNGRY bear with an appetite will eat up any food in sight.

And all bears hate baked beans on toast

But love ripe hares and rabbits the most!

Rabbit quickly grabbed Hare's paw.
"Run for it, Hare! It's lucky those bears
have never read your book. If they did,
I bet they'd try to make a hare and
rabbit pie!"

Little Mouse and the Big Red Apple

by A. H. Benjamin

Illustrated by
John Bendall-Brunello

Mouse was feeling hungry one day,
when all of a sudden he came across
a big, red, juicy apple.

"Just what I want!" he cried.
"I'll take it home with me and have
a feast!"

Mouse set off toward his little house,
rolling the apple over and over.

He couldn't wait to get his teeth into
the big, red, juicy apple. *Yum, yum*, he
thought, when all of a sudden . . .

SPLASH!

. . . the apple rolled into a pond.
"Oh, no!" wailed Mouse.
"What am I going to do now?"
"Not to worry," said Frog,
popping his head out of the
water. "I'll help you."

Frog kicked the apple hard
with his strong back legs.
It flew out of the water, and . . .

BUMP!

landed on the ground.
"There you are," said Frog.
He licked his lips and
stared at the apple.

"Er, thanks," said Mouse, as he began to roll it along the path. He did not want to share his apple with Frog. Mouse went on his way, thinking of the delicious apple dinner he would have later. His mouth was already watering when . . .

CRASH!

the big, red, juicy
apple fell into a
thorn bush.

"Silly me!" muttered
Mouse, as he tried to
rescue his dinner.
"Ouch, that hurt!"
he cried. "Those
prickles are sharp!"

"I see you have a problem," said Tortoise,
moving next to Mouse. "Leave it to me."
Tortoise didn't have to worry about
the sharp prickles. He had his shell
to protect him.

Without any trouble
at all, Tortoise crept
under the thorn bush and
brought out the big, red, juicy apple.
"Problem solved!" he said, stroking
the apple longingly.

"Thank you so much," said
Mouse in a hurried voice, and he
was off again. He did not want to
share his apple with Tortoise.
*I'll soon be home and biting
into that big, red, juicy apple,*
thought Mouse, when . . .

the apple rolled into a log.

"That's all I need!" sighed Mouse when
he saw that the log blocked his path.
"How do I get around that?"

"Easy!" said Mole, popping out of a nearby hole. "I'll dig you a tunnel."

And she did. She dug a tunnel that went right under the log.

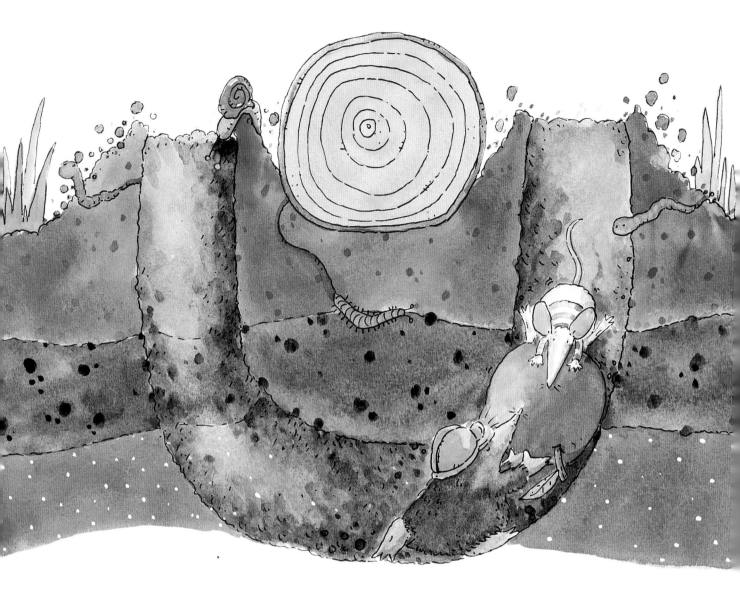

It was just wide enough for Mouse
and the apple to go through it.

"Always glad to help!" said Mole, sniffing at the big, red, juicy apple with her little nose.

"It's very kind of you," said Mouse, and he went on his way as fast as he could. He did not want to share the apple with Mole. He rolled the apple over and over until . . .

. . . he came
to a steep hill.
His house was at
the very top.

PUSH

Push, push,
heave, heave,
went Mouse,
grunting and
groaning.

PUSH

HEAVE

HEAVE

Up, up, up
he went,
until he reached
the very top.

"At last!" sighed
Mouse happily.
"Oh, for that wonderful
apple meal!" But as
Mouse let go . . .

. . . the apple wobbled,
and then it started
to roll . . .

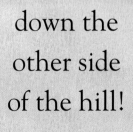

down the
other side
of the hill!

It rolled
faster and
faster…

further
and further,
until…

. . . it came to a stop at the bottom of the hill. Mouse could see it lying there, like a big red jewel.

"Oh, no," he cried. "I'll have to start all over again!"

Mouse scrambled down the hill on his
little tired feet. Faster and faster he ran . . .

. . . but when he reached the bottom he found
Frog, Mole, and Tortoise had gotten there first!
"How kind of you to send that apple
all the way back to us," called
out Mole, chomping
away on a piece
of it.

Mouse gave a
big, big sigh. "Don't
mention it," he said.
"Isn't that what friends
are for?"

The Nutty Nut Chase

by Kathryn White   Illustrated by Vanessa Cabban

Hickory was making rude faces at Pecan
when the strangest thing happened.

POP!

A shiny brown nut suddenly burst up from the ground. It wobbled and shook, wibbled and quivered, then lay there, teasingly delicious.

"Wow, lunch!" Pecan shouted.

"Wow, lunch and dinner!" Hickory screeched.

"It's my nut," said Pecan.

"It's mine!" snapped Hickory.

"Who's making that noise?" shouted Badger.
"I'm trying to sleep."
    All the animals came out to see what
was happening.

"My nut!" Pecan shouted.

"It's mine!" yelled Hickory. "I saw it first."

"Did not."

"Did so."

"Pull his ears!" shouted Littlest Rabbit.

"Certainly not. Pulling ears doesn't solve problems," said Badger firmly.

"Oh," said Littlest Rabbit, disappointed. "Then bop his nose."

"No pulling or bopping," said Badger. "There will be a competition, and the winner will get the nut."

"I know," said Hedgehog. "The prickliest wins the nut."

"But you're the prickliest," said Pecan and Hickory.

"So I am!" said Hedgehog, delighted. "I win! I get the nut."

"Cuddliest gets the nut," said Littlest Rabbit. "I win!"

"Enough!"

said Badger. "We will have a
race. First to reach the tree wins."

"Hooray, a race!" everyone cheered.

Blackbird whistled the
start of the race. They were off!
Pecan and Hickory shot ahead,
but the rabbits were close behind.
Hedgehog tried to run but only managed
a waddle. In a huff, he curled himself into
a ball and rolled full speed down the slope.
Littlest Rabbit looked back to see a prickly
ball spinning toward them. "Look out!"
he called. But it was too late!

Hedgehog crashed through
the racers like a cannonball
and everyone landed in a
prickly heap.

"Oh, dear," tutted Badger.
"We'll have to start again.
And prickly cannonballs
aren't allowed."

Hedgehog snorted
and sulked off.

Blackbird whistled, and they were off again.

Pecan and Hickory were neck and neck.

"My nut!" shouted Pecan triumphantly. "I win!"

"No!" shouted Hickory. "It's mine! I win!"

Suddenly, the nut began to move. It twitched and jerked, joggled and jiggled until PLOP! it disappeared down under the ground.

"It's a magic nut!" shouted Littlest Rabbit.

"Nutty magic!" squealed Hedgehog, racing back to see.

"Bet it would have tasted magic, too," said Shrew.

POP!

The nut sprang up
right in front of Shrew.

"Quick, grab it!" shouted Littlest Rabbit.

All the animals shot across the grass, rolling
and shrieking, jumping and hopping, banging and
bopping into each other.

"I've got it!" shouted Hedgehog, but the nut
vanished again.

"That's my nose!" Shrew squeaked.

"Shhhhh!" said Badger suddenly. "Look."

He pointed at the magic nut that had appeared at his feet. Everyone tiptoed up to it. The nut shook and quivered. The animals looked in amazement.

"Help!" squealed the nut.

"AAAH!" shrieked Littlest Rabbit. "A talking nut."

"You're a talking nut," said Pecan.

Heeeelp!

Pecan and Hickory bent down and pulled
and tugged, yanked and wrenched at the
nut with all their might.

Out flew the nutshell, sending Pecan
and Hickory rolling backward. And there,
where the nut had been, was Mole!

POP!

Mole shook himself and stood up on his two tiny legs. "Thanks!" he said. "I thought I would be stuck in that nutshell for ever."

Littlest Rabbit put the empty shell on his head. "It makes a great hat," he giggled.

"That looked like the tastiest nut ever," groaned Pecan and Hickory.

"There's plenty more where that came from," chirped Mole, and he disappeared underground.

Suddenly, shiny nuts began
popping up all over the place.
"There's enough for everyone!"
Mole chuckled.

POP!

POP!

"Magic!" shouted Hickory.
"Magic!" shouted Pecan.
"Nutty magic!" everyone shouted,
and they all munched with delight.

POP!

POP!

YUCK!
That's Not a Monster!

by Angela McAllister
Illustrated by Alison Edgson

Mr. and Mrs. Monster were very proud of their three eggs.

Mr. Monster kept them warm by huffing with his hot, stinky breath.

Mrs. Monster screeched to them.

One stormy night,
the first egg cracked.
Out climbed an ugly little
monster, with prickly spikes
and snarly fangs.
"Aaah! He's FRIGHTFUL!"
sighed Mr. and
Mrs. Monster happily.
So that's what they
called him.

Then the second
egg cracked. Out climbed another
ugly little monster, with spiky spines
and bristly warts.
"Oooh! She's HORRID!"
gasped Mr. and Mrs. Monster
happily. So that's what
they called her.

Then the third egg shook a bit. Frightful
and Horrid gave it a poke. Out crept
something very soft and pink.
"UGH! HE'S SWEET!!"
said the little monsters.
"LET'S SQUASH HIM!"

"Well, he's not what we expected," said Mrs. Monster. "He is a bit of a shock."

"Let's throw him in the garbage can," said Mr. Monster.

Suddenly, there was a crash of thunder.

"Mama!" cried the fluffy one and jumped into Mrs. Monster's arms.

She looked down at her bundle of sweetness. "I think we'll keep him," she said. "He may look different but inside he is a monster, just like us." So they called him Little Shock.

Each day, Frightful
and Horrid grew hairier
and scarier.

They learned how to spit
and hiss and snarl and
scratch.

But Little Shock grew MORE
fluffy. He liked to gurgle and roly-poly
and twinkle his big blue eyes. He loved
his brother and sister and followed
them everywhere.

AWOOOOOOOOOOO!

"If you want to play with us, you've got to be wild and scary," said Frightful and Horrid. They showed him how to howl at the moon until it hid behind a cloud. But Little Shock was afraid of the dark.

They showed him how to squash and
stamp and trample. But Little Shock saw a
worried worm and sat down to give it a hug.
"Ugh!" sneered Frightful and Horrid.
"He's just a cutie-pie!"

Soon Frightful and Horrid were bold enough
to go monstering in the woods by themselves.
"You must take your brother with you,"
insisted Mrs. Monster.

Frightful and Horrid snorted grumpily,
but they put Little Shock in a wagon, hid
him under a blanket, and tugged him along.

In the woods, Frightful leapt out
at a fox and made its fur turn white.
Horrid pounced on a wild pig and
made it jump into a tree.
They had a wonderful time!

GRRR!

RARGH!

Little Shock cuddled his blanket
and played peekaboo with a mouse.

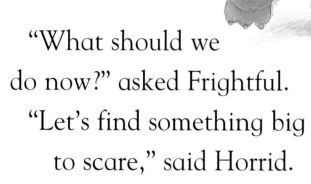

"What should we
do now?" asked Frightful.
"Let's find something big
to scare," said Horrid.

Something big rustled in the bushes
ahead, so they crept up on it. Frightful
and Horrid saw a hairy hump. They
winked at each other, took a deep
breath, and . . .

But the hairy hump was only a little bit of a BIG monster! It snarled and flashed its fiery eyes. "WHO DARED TO ROAR AT ME?"

Frightful and Horrid were too terrified to run away. Their spines shriveled and their claws curled up.

Suddenly, the BIG monster spotted Little Shock.

"OOOH! COTTON CANDY!" he said.

Little Shock stared up at the monster's face. His big blue eyes grew wider and wider . . .

Then MUAH!
He gave the monster
a kiss right on
the cheek!

"YUCK!"

The BIG monster wailed and dropped
Little Shock in horror. He was so afraid that
his fur turned to frizz and his bristles fell out.

"HELP!" he cried. "IT'S
ADORABLE!"
And he ran away, crying
for his mommy.

Frightful and Horrid
couldn't believe
their eyes.
"You kissed him!
You kissed him!"
they laughed.

Horrid swung her little brother high in the air and sat him on Frightful's shoulders.

"Maybe being cute could be useful after all," she said, giving him a pinch.

Little Shock just purred happily.

"Come on, then," said Frightful proudly. "Let's go home and ALL kiss Mom and Dad!"

The Little Lost Robin

by Elizabeth Baguley

Illustrated by Tina Macnaughton

On the edge of the deep wood lived an old hare. Once, he had leapt and pranced under the magical moon, but time had made him gray and stiff, and he no longer danced. Instead, he spent his time looking out over the world, gently daydreaming.

Every day, Hare went to feed the small
brown birds, who chattered and chirruped.
Remembering his long-ago moondancing,
Hare tapped a merry paw to their busy tunes.
One morning, in swooped a bird with
a berry-bright breast. "You're a bold little
robin," laughed Hare.

Even when autumn came, Hare still went
to share food with his friends. But then
a chill wind scattered the leaves, and the
birds, too cold to stay, flew far away.

Their song echoed with good-bye.

"I'll miss you, little birds," sighed Hare.

Then something made Hare prick up his ears.
A song! A song that lilted faintly, away in the
woods. It was a bird! Hare hurried toward the
fir tree where Robin shone scarlet, singing a
song warm as summer.

"Robin! You didn't fly away!" exclaimed Hare.

And as Robin sang brightly, Hare spun around in a slow dance.

"You've made this old hare feel young again," he laughed.

So, every day, Hare would walk into the blustery woods to bring Robin seeds and sway to her song.

When winter arrived, freezing the woods and stiffening Hare's legs, Robin would come to the burrow to see him. Hare would wake up as soon as the sun rose, and wait for her so that they could eat breakfast together.

"What would I do without you?" smiled Hare.

Then came a night that howled with storm-fury. A wild wind exploded into the woods, blasting and splintering trees. In whirled the snow, hiding the land under its biting cold whiteness.

Deep in his burrow, Hare could not sleep because he was worried about Robin. Had she been blown into the storm, homeless and afraid?

At first light Hare rushed outside, hoping that Robin would be waiting for him. But there was no Robin, no Robin anywhere! Where was she? Why hadn't she come? Hare had to try to find her.

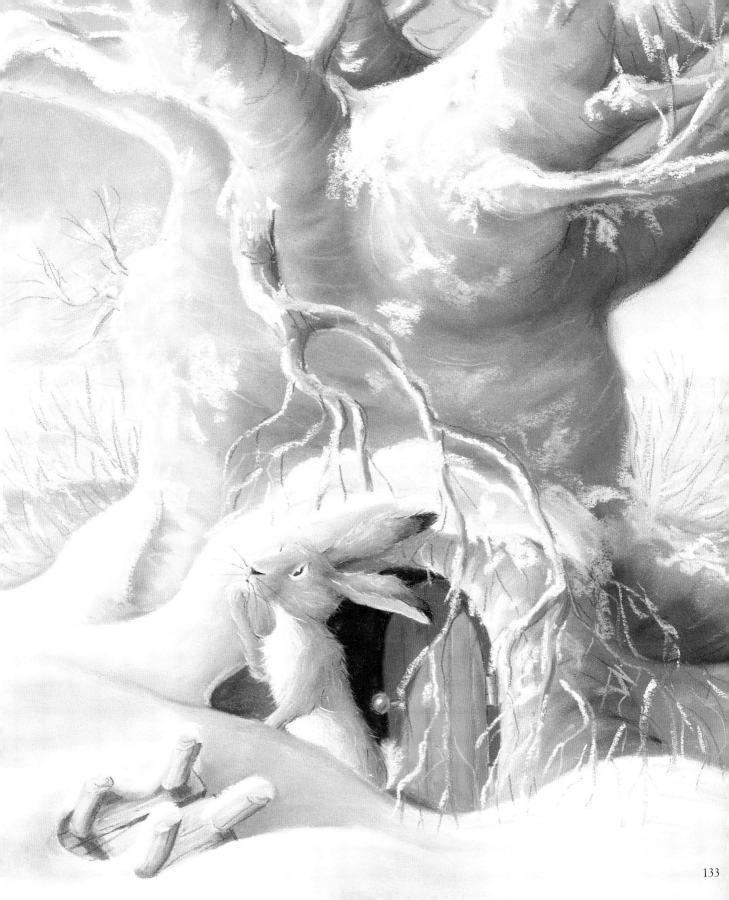

Out into the snowy woods
Hare struggled. Finally he
came to Robin's tree and
stopped. It lay fallen, wrenched
from the ground by the storm.
"Robin!" he gasped. "Where are you?"
But searching through the
branches, Hare found only
her empty nest.

He slumped down, sure
that Robin was lost.

Just then, a tiny cheep
made him look up.

"Robin!" Hare shouted in
amazement. "I thought the
storm had taken you!"

As fast as she could, Robin flew to him.
"It's all right, little one," Hare said gently.
"You can come back with me. I'll plant your
tree outside my burrow, so you'll feel at home."

The sun sank slowly
as Hare trudged home.
Over the humps and
hollows of snow he went,
with Robin nestled safely
on his shoulder.

Back home, Hare helped Robin make a new nest
in the fir tree's branches. Every day she warbled
and whistled, and when the night brought the
light of the magical moon, Hare joyfully danced
to her winter-bright tunes.

Little Honey Bear
and the Smiley Moon

by Gillian Lobel　　Illustrated by Tim Warnes

Little Honey Bear couldn't sleep.
Through his bedroom window the
moon was shining, as bright as day.
The snowy woods glimmered in
the brilliant moonlight. And surely
the moon was smiling at him!

"Why, hello Moon!" cried
Little Bear. And he rushed out
into the glittering woods.

There in the moonlight was Lily Long Ears, making snow hares.

"Hello, Little Honey Bear," said Lily. "Couldn't you sleep either?"

"Oh, Lily," said Little Bear, "the moon sailed right in front of my window, and she smiled at me!"

"Me too!" said Lily. "She's so big and smiley tonight, I just had to come out to say hello."

She showered Little Bear with snow. "Catch me if you can!" she cried, and darted away through the trees.

They ran through the moonlit
woods into a wide snowy meadow.
High above hung the moon and
right across the frozen meadow
ran a shining silver pathway.

"It's a pathway to the moon!"
cried Little Bear. "Just think, Lily—
we could walk all the way to the
moon and say hello."

"Little Honey Bear," squeaked
a tiny voice. "Can I come, too?"

"'Course you can, Teeny Tiny
Mouse," said Little Bear.

So off along the moonpath
went the three friends.

"What will we do when we get to the moon?" asked Lily.

"We will have a snack," said Little Bear. "We will have mooncakes and moonjuice!"

"What are mooncakes like, Little Honey Bear?" asked Tiny Mouse.

"Why, they're round, and flat, and silvery," said Little Bear. "And very sweet, of course."

"Let's go then!" squeaked Tiny Mouse.

Suddenly the night grew colder. A crisp wind whipped the snow into little flurries. The path to the moon grew steeper and steeper.

"It's an awful long way to the moon," gasped Tiny Mouse. "My little paws are freezing."

So Little Bear scooped Tiny Mouse into his paw, and set him on his big shoulder.

"That's much better!" said Tiny Mouse, tucking his toes into Little Bear's thick furry coat. "My paws are happy now."

Up and up ran the moonpath toward
the very top of the hill. Snowflakes stung
their eyes and whirled into their ears.

"Do you think we'll get there soon,
Little Honey Bear?" gasped Lily.
"My ears are getting cold!"
    As she spoke, a great cloud blew in
front of the moon . . .

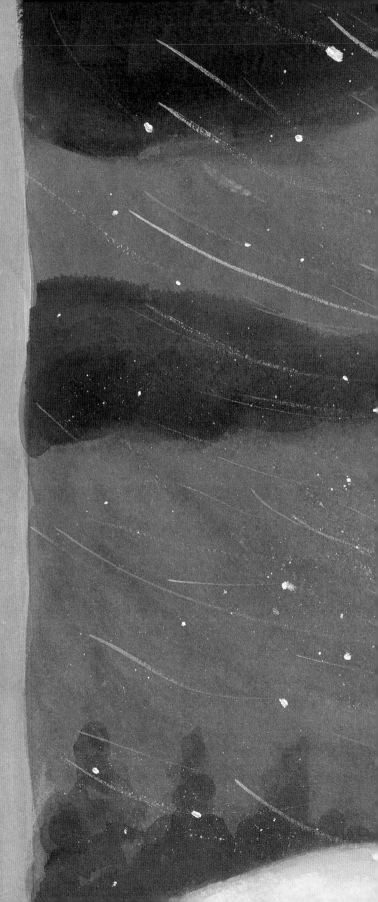

. . . and the moonpath disappeared. Suddenly, it was very dark.

"I don't like it, Little Honey Bear," said Lily. "I don't like it at all!"

"I d-d-don't think I want to go to the moon after all," said Tiny Mouse. "Even for mooncakes."

So off they set down the hill.

Down and down they slipped and slithered, until they reached the woods.

"Maybe the moon is angry and doesn't want to see us after all," said Little Honey Bear.

"I want to go home," quavered Tiny Mouse.

"Me too!" gasped Lily.

But everything looked
different in the dark,
and they couldn't find
their way home.

The trees creaked and
groaned, and the woods
were full of shadows.
"I think we're lost,"
sniffed Little Bear. "And
I want my mommy!"

Suddenly, a silvery light
flooded the woods. And
up above, bobbing between
the trees, the smiling moon
appeared.

"Hooray!" cried everyone.
And then the moonlight
fell upon a big furry bear,
her arms open wide as she
ran toward them.

"Oh, Little Honey Bear,
I'm so glad I've found you!"
cried Mommy Bear. And
she gave them all a very
big bear hug.

"Oh, Mommy," said Little Bear. "We were going to have a snack with the moon, but then she got angry with us, and hid."

"And we didn't get to drink moonjuice," sighed Tiny Mouse.

"Or taste mooncakes," said Lily sadly.

Mother Bear smiled as she took them all back to the warm bear house for a special moon supper, with golden honey cakes and warm milk to drink.

"The moon wasn't angry. She was there all along," she said. "The clouds were hiding her!"

"Mommy," said Little Bear later,
as she tucked him up in his bed,
"I really wanted to go
and see the moon."

"Why, Little Bear, we
don't need to go to the moon
to see her—she's all around us!"

Little Honey Bear looked through the window. Every tree was hung with a thousand glassy rainbows in the bright moonlight. And then the moon sailed through the trees and smiled at him.

"Good night, Moon," said Little Bear, rubbing his eyes. Then he turned over and fell fast asleep.

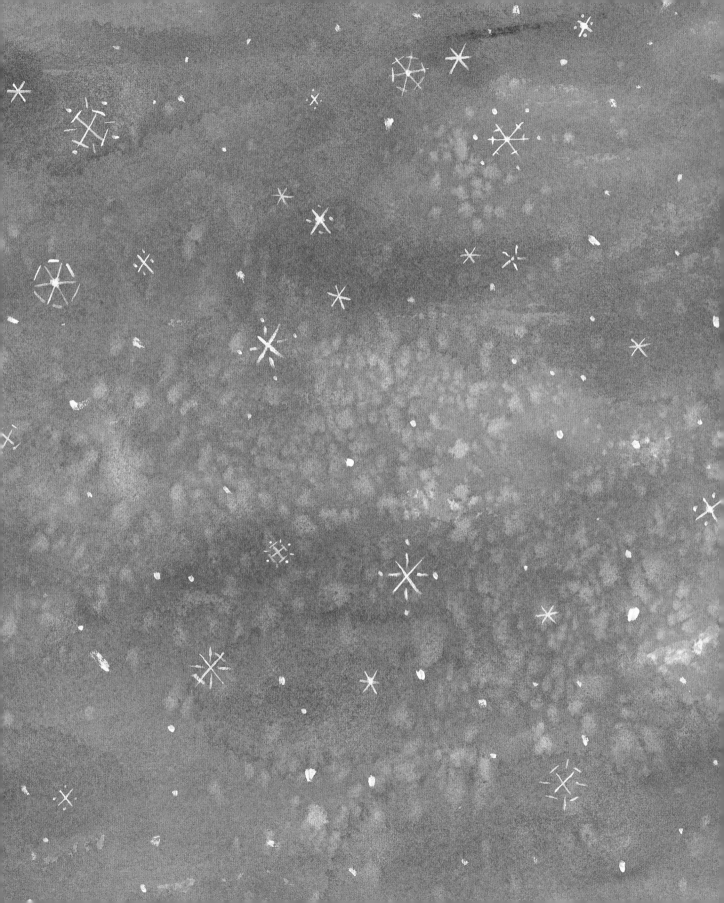

STORIES TO SHARE

tiger tales
5 River Road, Suite 128, Wilton, CT 06897
Published in the United States 2015
First published in Great Britain 2015 by Little Tiger Press
This volume copyright © 2015 Little Tiger Press
Cover artwork copyright © 2006 Tim Warnes,
2000 Gwyneth Williamson, 2007 Alison Edgson
ISBN-13: 978-1-58925-537-1
ISBN-10: 1-58925-537-2
Printed in China • LTP/1800/0982/0914
All rights reserved
10 9 8 7 6 5 4 3 2 1

For more insight and activities,
visit us at www.tigertalesbooks.com

FOLLOW THAT BEAR IF YOU DARE!

by Claire Freedman
Illustrated by Alison Edgson

First published in Great Britain 2007
by Little Tiger Press

Text copyright © 2007 Claire Freedman
Illustrations copyright © 2007 Alison Edgson

LITTLE MOUSE AND THE BIG RED APPLE

by A. H. Benjamin
Illustrated by Gwyneth Williamson

First published in Great Britain 2000
by Little Tiger Press

Text copyright © 2000 A. H. Benjamin
Illustrations copyright © 2000 Gwyneth Williamson

THE NUTTY NUT CHASE

by Kathryn White
Illustrated by Vanessa Cabban

First published in Great Britain 2004
by Little Tiger Press

Text copyright © 2004 Kathryn White
Illustrations copyright © 2004 Vanessa Cabban

YUCK! THAT'S NOT A MONSTER!

by Angela McAllister
Illustrated by Alison Edgson

First published in Great Britain 2010
by Little Tiger Press

THE LITTLE LOST ROBIN

by Elizabeth Baguley
Illustrated by Tina Macnaughton

First published in Great Britain 2007
by Little Tiger Press

LITTLE HONEY BEAR AND THE SMILEY MOON

by Gillian Lobel
Illustrated by Tim Warnes

First published in Great Britain 2006
by Little Tiger Press